Dylan's Day

by Tim Hutchinson

Dylan's Day

Text © 2013 by Tim Hutchinson
Illustrations © 2013 by Tim Hutchinson

Pinwheel Books
www.pinwheelbooks.com

Library of Congress Control Number: 2013902682
ISBN-13: 978-0-9854248-1-7

Dylan's Day

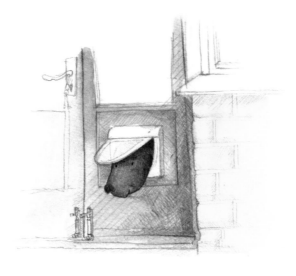

by Tim Hutchinson

For Jo
For Mum and Dad
T.H.

Dylan stretches and yawns. Today there are important things to do, like checking the bed to see if the sleep has gone.

ut what is most important and needs doing is finding that big fat
at that lives next door.

Today there are important things to sniff, like bread and window
and where a bluebird sits.

ut what is most important and needs sniffing most is the big fat
at that lives next door.

Today there are a
lot of things to find,
like soap . . .

and some old rope...

and a watering can.

But what is most important and must be found is the big fat cat
that lives next door.

nd there are important things to follow,

like bees...

and balls...

and big butterflies.

And things to chase, like a red robin,

a magpie, and a sparrow...

...and also Mrs. Grumpy Face
from number 24.

ut what is more important and simply must be chased is the big
t cat that lives next door.

So Dylan searches for hours, digging up flowers and tipping over pots and old paint tins.

He looks outside and in...

under the bed...

he looks everywhere...

Even in the garden shed.

Where is that big fat cat that lives next door?
He searches and searches, and searches some more.

Dylan sits and thinks very hard.
But as he thinks, he hears the loudest noise!

Oh what a fright!
Oh what a sight is the big fat cat from next door!

ylan runs as fast as he can, down the garden path and into the
afe, warm house.

There he snuggles under his blanket and decides that what simply must be done...

...is going to bed and forgetting that big fat cat that lives next door

The End

CPSIA information can be obtained
at www.ICGtesting.com
Printed in the USA
LVIC04n0942270414
383362LV00004B/4